Brothers

OF THE

KNIGHT

DEBBIE ALLEN

pictures by KADIR NELSON

Brothers
OF THE
KNIGHT

SCHOLASTIC INC.

New York Toronto London Auckland Sydney
Mexico City New Delhi Hong Kong Buenos Aires

Once upon a time in a little village called Harlem, that's in New York City, there lived a man, Reverend Knight. Spelled with a *K*, like knight in shining armor. And like a knight, he was a very good man, a leader in the community, who preached a powerful sermon every Sunday. He lived with his twelve sons, whom he loved with all his heart . . .

Reverend Knight

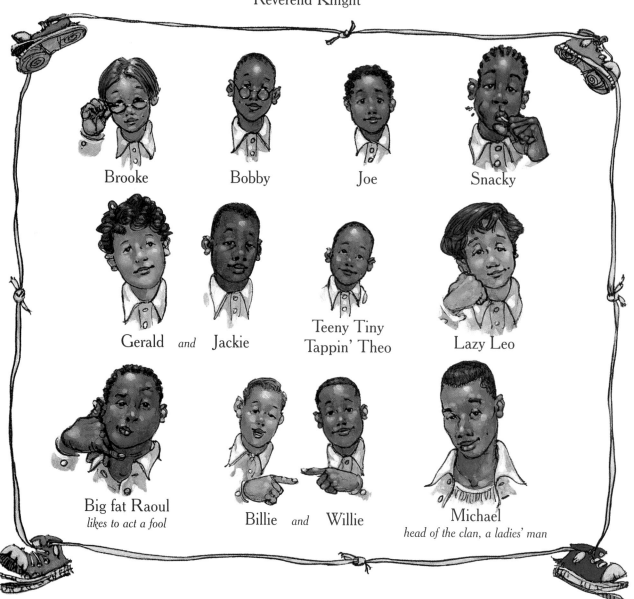

Brooke

Bobby

Joe

Snacky

Gerald   *and*   Jackie

Teeny Tiny
Tappin' Theo

Lazy Leo

Big fat Raoul
likes to act a fool

Billie   *and*   Willie

Michael
head of the clan, a ladies' man

and their big dog, Happy! That's me! That's right, I'm a talking dog. It's a magical story. (You didn't say anything when that pig was talking in that movie . . . quiet!) Reverend Knight raised his sons with a firm, loving hand . . . but a lot was goin' on that couldn't be explained.

Well, the trouble all started when every housekeeper Reverend Knight hired either quit or got fired. Why? Because every morning the brothers' shoes would be worn to threads, messed up, torn up, stinky, dirty, tacky, jacked up . . . you get the picture. And you *know* they tried to blame it on me. Oh! The dog did it. The dog! What did I want with some ol' stinkin' shoes? And let me tell you, that little one's feet smelled worse than all of 'em. Phew!

Reverend Knight gave all the nannies a key to lock the brothers in at night. Lizzie, the last nanny, even tried puttin' slip-and-slide wax on the floor, so if anybody got up in the middle of night, they'd make a lot of noise. The only noise we heard was when her big butt fell down and broke the floor. Ha! Well, that's another story. But every night not one peep could be heard from the brothers' room, and they would be sound asleep the next morning. Still, every morning their shoes would be worn to threads, messed up, torn up, stinky, dirty, tacky, jacked up. . . . And if you asked those boys about their shoes, they said that they had slept all night, but they had fun in their dreams.

Reverend was at his wits' end. People came from far and wide to hear his sermons, and yet he couldn't solve the problems in his own home. One day Reverend Knight put a big two-page ad in *Jet* magazine.

WANTED: HOUSEKEEPER
EXPERIENCED WITH BOYS 7 TO 17,
BONUS TRIP TO JAMAICA IF TORN-UP
SHOES MYSTERY IS SOLVED.

Yes, I can read too.

That Sunday he preached a powerful sermon, had the people really feeling the spirit. But he didn't let them do too much shoutin'. Thought it was undignified.

After the congregation filed out and the brothers went to choir practice, he went into his private room and prayed for guidance and help with his sons. Where do I go from here? he asked over and over.

When the brothers and Reverend Knight returned home from church, a small woman dressed in bright colors was waiting on their doorstep. She talked like a sweet bird. Said, "I've come to help with the boys. My name is Sunday, sweet Sunday, because I bake pies and cakes." She had lots of energy, and all her belongings fit in one small bag that was so heavy, even Reverend couldn't pick it up.

Sunday took one look at the house, opened her bag, and pulled out all kinds of mops and brooms. She put the brothers to work cleaning. Dusting, waxing, mopping, washing windows till they sparkled and shined. The brothers didn't like it one bit.

Reverend Knight liked her very much. Ooh, talk about cookin'! Her smothered chicken, sweet potato biscuits, and lemon crunch cookies were jump up and down, slap yo' own self in the face good! After dinner that night, with the brothers eavesdropping on the grown folks' conversation, Reverend confided that he really hoped that she could solve the mystery of the torn-up shoes. "There's something going on that the boys won't tell me."

Sunday, taking him by the hand, replied, "Rest your mind, Reverend. I'm sure the brothers will learn to trust me and tell me everything."

Reverend sighed and leaned back on the couch with a big ol' smile on his face.

The brothers weren't having any of that! The oldest, Michael, said, "Let's put her to the test just like all the rest." The brothers put their hands together and made a pact. "Ol' girl's gotta go!"

The brothers slept together in one *loooong* bed. Soon as Reverend tucked them in that evening and said good night, the door was locked. Sunday went right to sleep on the other side of the door. She was snoring like a little bear when the Cookie Man sneaked through the secret doorway in their bed. "Party time!" he yelled, sounding like an elf, 'cause that's exactly what he was.

The brothers, tiptoeing quietly, got dressed, grabbed their dancing
canes, and sneaked out through the secret doorway. They didn't know
that Sunday had been sleeping with one eye open. She pulled a magic
scarf that made her invisible out of her small bag and followed along.

The brothers danced their way 'cross the rooftops. Steppin' and stompin'. The moon gave everything a magical glow, as if they were dancing on the Milky Way.

Still invisible, Sunday followed them down a fire escape, down a
shiny pole, to the Big Band Ballroom, the liveliest dance spot in
the world. The girls were already there, waiting for the brothers to
show. . . . Ooo, talk about a party!

Sunday watched as each brother matched up with his girl. Even
Tiny Tappin' Theo had a partner, Charlotte. Theo told me Charlotte
was phat! You know, good lookin'. He doesn't know what phat is.
Nadine, that big Irish setter down the street, now that's phat! Anyway,
as I was saying . . . Each couple seemed to out-dance the other *swingin'*.

By the end of the night everybody's shoes were worn to threads, messed up, torn up, stinky, dirty, tacky, jacked up. And just before the sun came up, they all dashed out of the Ballroom.

Sunday ran ahead of them 'cross the rooftops . . . the brothers
followed. Sunday hurried through the secret passage . . . and by the
time the brothers got back, she was snoring like a little bear on the
other side of their door.

The brothers piled their worn-out shoes in front of their bed and went to sleep. Sunday snuck back into the room. Swirling her magic scarf, she said, "Wooh Great Googah Moogah Sugah Boogah." And she made the torn-up shoes vanish and brand-new ones appear.

When Reverend came in to wake the boys, he found all their shoes in front of the bed, clean and sparkling. Sunday was up and cheerful, hurryin' them to come and eat breakfast. She had baked special biscuits shaped like shoes. Snacky whispered to Michael, "We better keep an eye on ol' girl."

Every night for a month the brothers would sneak out to the Ballroom. Every night Sunday, invisible in her magic scarf, would follow. And every morning their shoes would sparkle, brand-new. They checked to make sure she was sleeping before they left and after they got home, and there she was, snoring like a little bear. They knew she'd been following them, but they didn't know how. Their father was just plain happy. The house was never cleaner, he never ate better (and neither did I), and there were no more torn-up shoes. Best of all, Sunday's sweetness was workin' a little magic on him. "How do you keep those boys' shoes so clean?" he'd ask her, looking a little starry-eyed. And she'd answer, "Oh, I just stay close to them, without getting in their way."

Finally the brothers waited for Sunday and got in her face.

Michael said, "We know you've been following us." Theo begged, "Please don't tell Dad."

Sunday said, "Boys, why do you keep this from him when he loves you so much?"

Michael answered, "Dad would never approve of us dancing like that. It doesn't fit with his image in the community."

Sunday said, "How do you know? You've never even talked with him about it."

Then Tiny Theo piped up, "Grown-ups are too old. You don't get kids, what we really like. Besides, none of you can dance anyway."

Joe echoed, "Yeah, Monday, you can't dance."

"My name is not Monday," she replied.

"Tuesday, whatever," said Joe as the brothers busted their sides laughing.

Well, Sunday broke into a dance routine that went from Jimmy
Slyde to Fred Astaire to Bob Fosse all the way to Michael Jackson.
  She kicked, jumped, and twirled all over that room. Taught us
all a thing or two. (That's right, I like to dance too!) The brothers
could hardly keep up with her, and laughed like crazy trying. And
that did it—they were friends. That night when the boys went to the
Ballroom, Sunday went too, and she didn't bother to wear her
magic scarf.

At breakfast the next morning, she started singing and tapping her feet as she served hot yellow grits. The brothers knew she was waiting for them to talk with their father. They weren't ready.

Then one evening Reverend Knight noticed me chewing on a torn-up, worn-out shoe. All right, all right, so I chew one up every once in a while! What are you gonna do, arrest me? I have to act like a dog sometimes just to make you people feel normal.

Anyway, Reverend looked and saw another chewed shoe by my foot and another by my tail. He followed the trail to the old pantry. Opened the door and there he saw the torn-up shoes piled high, almost to the ceiling! Well, how was I supposed to know? I'm just the dog. Oh, you people! That's right, always blamin' it on the dog. We lead such a hard life.

When Sunday and the brothers returned home from the movies, Reverend Knight was pacing back and forth in front of all those shoes. Sunday stared at the brothers, but they didn't say a word. So she stepped forward.

"Reverend, please don't blame the boys for keeping secrets from you. It's all my fault. I'll pack my things and leave tomorrow. But may I say one thing?"

He nodded.

"You have done a fine job raising your sons, but the truth is, they don't believe you really want to know how they feel, why they do—"

Reverend Knight interrupted her. "Thank you, Miss Sunday, I know my boys."

"Of course you do," said Sunday. "Good-bye, Reverend."

The thought of Sunday leaving pulled at the hearts of the father and the boys, but no one was ready to stand up for her except me. I howled and howled, but they just put me outside.

The next day, with tears in their eyes the brothers said good-bye
to Sunday. She kissed each one and, with her suitcase in hand, she
left for the bus station.

Reverend and the brothers went to church. Then, with the rays of the sun shining on his face, and the spirit of love touching his heart, Reverend gave the sermon of his life.

Looking right at his sons, he preached, shouted, and even started to prance. Talking about trusting in the Lord and remembering how to trust one another. He got carried away, and he did the twist, the mashed potato, and the monkey time. When he started the funky chicken, the whole congregation sprang to its feet and began to wail. The brothers shouted the loudest.

As soon as church was out, the boys rushed to their father. They told the whole story—how they loved to dance, and sneaked out to the Big Band Ballroom, but were afraid he wouldn't approve, and how Sunday had only tried to give them time to face their father.

Reverend hugged his sons and asked, "Can you forgive me for keeping something from you?"

The brothers looked puzzled.

Reverend Knight said, "I used to be the best dancer at the Sock Hops. Now we better hurry and try to get Sunday back."

Sunday was just getting ready to board the bus when Reverend
Knight, out of breath, knelt down right in the middle of the street.
"Sunday, will you dance with me?"

He told her how sorry he was, and how she needed to come
back home so they could be a family. The brothers surrounded her.
She had to say yes.

Well, let the church bells start ringing! The brothers were so happy, they all started dancing, and the people on the street started dancing . . . and chanting, "There's gonna be a wedding. There's gonna be a wedding."

I had to call my designer and get an outfit.

Sunday and Reverend were married, and had their reception
at the Big Band Ballroom. What a party that was!

Oh, and they all lived happily ever after . . . except me.

Treated me like a dog. Put me outside, 'cause somebody went
and gave them a cat. I'm tellin' you, you just can't trust people.

To my mother, Vivian Ayers,
and all the young boys who love to dance
D.A.

For Keara and Amel
K.N.

ISBN 0-439-36703-4

12 11 10 9 8 7 6 5 4 3   3 4 5 6 7 8/0

Designed by Pamela Darcy

Printed in the U.S.A.   24

First Scholastic printing, January 2003

For each full-color painting, a pencil drawing was created, which was photocopied.
Oil paints were then applied to the photocopy.